PIRATE PRINCESS

POPPY

JUDY BROWN

SIMON AND SCHUSTER

SIMON AND SCHUSTER

First published in Great Britain by Simon and Schuster UK Ltd, 2008
A CBS COMPANY

1 3 5 7 9 10 8 6 4 2

Simon & Schuster UK Ltd
Africa House
64-78 Kingsway
London WC2B 6AH

A CIP catalogue record for this book is available from the British Library

ISBN: 978-1-41690-193-8

Printed and bound in Great Britain by Cox & Wyman Ltd, Reading, Berkshire

PIRATE PRINCESS

More adventures of the

PIRATE PRINCESS

Portia

Pandora

Pancake

Contents

King Colin and Queen Bettina
are pleased to announce
the marriage of their daughter
Princess ~~Petticoat~~ Poppy
to
Crown Prince Englebert
of Appledorf
on Saturday May 4th in the Palace Gardens
R.S.V.P

Portia the Pirate Princess stood at the wheel of her pirate ship, the *Flying Pig*, and breathed in the fresh sea air.

'Morning, Cap'n!' said First Mate Jim, from the main deck.

'Morning, Jim!' replied Portia. 'And isn't it a lovely one too?' she beamed.

Portia had been sailing the seven seas in her pirate ship ever since she ran away from her life as a princess. She'd been stuck in a stuffy old palace and desperate not to be married off to the ghastly Prince Rupert. So Portia ran away with her ladies-in-waiting and sold her crown to buy a ship. Now there were four more princesses on board, all rescued from dull marriages to even duller princes by Portia and her crew. Any princess in peril could get in touch with Portia via 'Parrot Post' by answering her ad in the *Princess Daily News*.

'Parrot ahoy!' called Emily, the Ship's Lookout, from the crow's nest. 'Looks like Squawk's carrying a letter.'

'Parrot post! Parrot post!' squawked Squawk as he flew towards the ship. He glided elegantly around the main mast and landed gently on Portia's shoulder.

Portia took the note that was tied to Squawk's leg and unrolled it carefully. Peppermint and Pancake had heard Squawk return and appeared on the main deck.

'What is it?' asked Peppermint. 'Another rescue?'

'Looks like it,' Portia said, sounding a little unsure. 'Meet me in my cabin. Jim, Pandora, you come, too.'

'I'll bring some biscuits,' said Pancake. 'I just made a fresh batch.'

Portia rang the ship's bell.

'Attention everyone!' she announced. 'Get everything ship-shape and ready to sail.' Almost instantly, the *Flying Pig* was a hive of activity. Portia bounded down the stairs to the main deck and headed for her cabin. Peppermint, Pandora and Jim were already waiting for her, and they stood around her as she read the note.

Dear Portia   Castle Pimento

My name is Princess Poppy but you probably
remember me as 'Petticoat,' because that's what
you all called me at school, oh how we laughed!
Naughty Daddy has gone and promised that I
will marry awful Crown Prince Englebert! All
he ever does is practise Morris dancing, write
poems and collect buttons, and he doesn't even
like my darling brother, Derek.
PLEASE, PLEASE RESCUE ME!!!!!
I'll be ever so grateful. I've drawn a map of the
route of the Wedding Procession on the back of
this letter, to help you work out where to save
me. PLEASE HURRY! The wedding is in
TWO days!
Love and kisses
Princess Poppy xxx   P.T.O.

Pancake joined them just as Portia finished
reading.

'Did I hear you right? Did you say Princess

Poppy?' she asked, putting down a plate of delicious-smelling biscuits that were still warm. 'What on earth does she want rescuing for? I thought she loved being a princess.'

'Me, too,' agreed Peppermint, helping herself to a biscuit. 'That was why she got nicknamed "Petticoat". She always wore at least three petticoats so that her dresses stuck out further than anyone else's. She was the prissiest girl in the school as far as I remember.'

'Well', mused Portia, 'I must admit I'm a bit surprised to hear from her. Mind you, Prince Englebert is wetter than a wet weekend in Wetland, and if Petticoat, I mean Poppy, has written to us, she obviously wants to be rescued.

Jim, bring me the *A-Z of Palaces and Castles.*'

Jim went over to the bookcase and Portia turned the letter over to look at the map on the back.

'Excellent!' Portia said, smiling. 'It should be pretty easy to work out a rescue. This shows the *exact* route the procession will take.'

Jim brought the *A-Z of Palaces* to the table and Portia turned to the section on Princess Poppy's castle.

'Ah, here we are, Castle Pimento.'

Pandora looked at the pictures.

'That cliff could be tricky but I'm sure I can come up with something,' she said thoughtfully.

'OK, Jim! Set a course for Castle Pimento,' said Portia. 'Girls, we've a rescue to plan!'

Chapter Two

Two days later, the *Flying Pig* anchored close to the cliffs near Castle Pimento. Portia and the team of rescuers were preparing to row ashore.

'Are the disguises ready, Donnatella?'

'Yes, Cap'n,' replied Donnatella. 'The false beards are a bit itchy but they look great.'

Donnatella had made a costume for each member of the crew who was going ashore. She had sewn long robes out of sacks, and made beards out of wire, with the stuffing from some old horse hair pillows. Portia, Jim, Pandora, Peppermint, Able Seawoman Anisha, Bosun Betty and Ship's Lookout Emily made up the rescue party. They stood on the deck looking like a band of desert tribesmen.

'I think you'd better stay here this time,
Squawk. I don't think a beard would suit you!'
giggled Portia. 'Pandora, is all your equipment in
the dinghy?'
'Yes, Cap'n!'
'OK. If everyone's ready, let's go.'
The boat was lowered into the water.

'It's going to be quite a climb up that cliff, especially with the stuff we'll have to carry,' said Portia, as they rowed towards the shore. 'I think Emily should go first. She's the best at climbing.'

Emily smiled proudly and when the dinghy bumped against the cliff, she was out of it and on her way up the cliff face in a flash.

'Watch where I put my feet,' she said, 'and try and follow.'

Half an hour later, they all reached the top, arms aching from the effort. Portia took out the map she had copied from Poppy's letter.

'Right,' she said, 'Pandora stay here and set up the equipment, and we'll meet you back here with Princess Poppy.' They all nodded. 'This way everyone,' Portia said, marching off purposefully.

It wasn't long before they heard the sound of music and crowds of happy people. As they reached the top of the hill, they could see the Royal Wedding Procession progressing along its route. Crown Prince Englebert was riding a white charger, its saddle blanket decorated with buttons, sewn on by the prince himself! About one

hundred metres behind followed Princess Poppy, seated in the Royal Procession Chair, a large, very ornamental sedan chair, which was carried by four footmen. The curtains were drawn round the princess, so that the prince didn't see her wedding dress before the ceremony. But her dainty hand waved a lace hanky at the crowds through the window. The streets were beautifully decorated and it seemed that everyone in the kingdom had turned out to cheer the royal couple on their way to the ceremony.

'It'll be easy to stay hidden in that crowd,' said Portia, sounding relieved. 'We'll weave our way through to that bend up ahead and that's where we'll pounce. Peppermint, have you got your sack of marbles?'

'Yes, Cap'n,' smiled Peppermint.

'OK, team, let's weave.'

They made their way through the crowds undetected and lay in wait as planned at the bend in the road. They joined in with the crowds, waving enthusiastically as the Prince passed by. They waited for his part of the Wedding Procession to disappear around the bend then, as Poppy's Royal Procession Chair approached, Portia signalled to the others.

'Ready?! One, two, three, GO!!!'

They all jumped out in front of the Chair shouting and waving their arms frantically.

'Stop the Procession!' yelled Portia. 'There's an ambush up ahead!'

There was a stunned silence and, as the footmen dropped the Royal Procession Chair in surprise, a loud 'Ooof!' came from inside. The crowd of people turned to look down the road and, quick as a flash, Jim, Betty, Emily and Anisha took hold of the chair and ran off as fast as they could, knocking the footmen off their feet. As the dazed footmen scrambled to get up, the crowd suddenly realised what was going on.

'Get them!' said one of the footmen. 'They're stealing the princess!'

'Marbles, Peppermint!' Portia commanded, and Peppermint ran forward, scattering marbles at the feet of the crowd as they tried to give chase. Everyone went flying.

Portia and Peppermint followed their
crewmates up the steep hill, scattering more
marbles behind them. They caught up with the
others sooner than they expected.

'How can one princess be *so* heavy?!' wheezed
Jim, as they struggled to the top of the hill with
the Royal Procession Chair.

'She must be made of lead!' groaned Bosun Betty.

Inside the curtained Chair, Princess Poppy was not enjoying the bumpy ride.

'I say!' she complained. 'You out there... ummph... could we go a little more carefully? All this jiggling around is messing up my hair. Ow!'

Jim tripped on the rocky ground and the ride got bumpier.

'I think we'd better lend a hand,' said Portia.

She and Peppermint poured the rest of the marbles down the hill, then they too grabbed hold of the Chair.

'You're right, this is heavy!' Portia winced.

'Maybe it's made of solid gold or something,' suggested Anisha.

Ten uncomfortable minutes later, they arrived back at the cliff top and collapsed speechless with exhaustion. The Chair went down with a bump. Another impatient 'Ooomph!' came from inside.

'Why have we stopped? Are we there already?' asked Poppy.

Nobody could answer.

Pandora had been very busy in their absence. She'd rigged up a system of pulleys to lower the Royal Procession Chair to the waiting dinghy. She looked at the rest of the rescue party, who were puffing and panting around her.

'What's wrong with you lot?' she asked, puzzled.

Portia tried to speak.

'Very ... puff ... heavy ... puff ... big ... puff ... hill ... wheeze!' she panted.

'People ... coming,' puffed Peppermint, pointing.

They struggled to pick up the Royal Procession Chair one more time, which wasn't quite so difficult now they weren't climbing a hill.

They secured it to the pulley mechanism and swung it around so that it dangled over the cliff.

'The rest of you go down the ropes. Peppermint and I will stay with the Chair,' said Portia, as she and Peppermint climbed on the roof.

Before long the rest of the rescue team had reached the dinghy and they began to lower the Chair down towards the sea. Suddenly, Princess Poppy realised that although the ride had become a lot less bumpy, something strange was going on. It felt as though she were travelling straight down! At last she poked her head out through the curtain to see what was happening.

'Ayeeeeek!' she screamed. 'I'm falling into the sea!'

'Don't be silly,' said Portia. 'You're perfectly safe.'

'Aaaaaaagh! Who are you?' Poppy shrieked, looking up at Portia and Peppermint. 'Help! HELP! I'm being princess-napped!'

'What are you talking about, you silly twit?' said Portia. Suddenly remembering she was still wearing a false beard, she took it off. 'It's me, Portia. We're rescuing you, like you asked us to.'

'How DARE you speak to me like that. I didn't asked to be rescued. I *like* being a princess. Take me back RIGHT NOW!'

Portia, baffled, looked at Peppermint.

'Perhaps she's just got cold feet?' suggested Peppermint, also taking off her beard.

'Well, it's too late to go back now,' said Portia.
'We'd be caught.

Poppy started to cry,

'Boo hoo! I want my mummy. I want to
go home.'

As the Royal Procession Chair descended, the
rest of the rescue team could hear what was
going on. They looked anxiously at Portia.

'Carry on, everyone,' said Portia sternly as the Chair touched down. 'We'll sort this mess out on board the ship.'

Pandora released the chair from the pulleys and they began to row back to the *Flying Pig*. The dinghy was silent except for a strange yapping noise and the snivels coming from Princess Poppy.

'What's going on, Cap'n?' asked Bosun Betty.

'I'm really not sure.' said Portia.

'And I still don't understand why that thing was so heavy,' said Jim, rubbing his tired arms. 'She doesn't look very big.'

'It's all very confusing,' Portia agreed, feeling a little uneasy.

Chapter Three

The Royal Procession Chair was heaved aboard the *Flying Pig* and Princess Poppy stumbled out of it and onto the deck. She was carrying a small hairy creature, which was obviously the source of the yapping.

'Shhhsh! Be quiet Froo-Froo,' said Poppy to the dog.

Twiggy, the ship's cat, emerged from her sleeping place. When she saw the yappy little thing, her fur stood on end. She tried to make herself look as big and scary as possible and hissed her biggest hiss.

Froo-Froo whimpered pathetically and jumped down to hide under his mistress's many petticoats.

'I remember you,' Poppy said to Portia, as she and the crew changed out of their rescue clothes. 'You're that Princess Portia from school. I never liked you then,' she added sulkily.

'Then why on earth did you write to me and ask to be rescued?!' shouted Portia, losing her temper.

'I keep telling you I DIDN'T. Why don't you listen, you ... you ... ignoramus!' Poppy shrieked, stamping her dainty little princess feet on the deck. 'Take me home RIGHT NOW! I won't stay on this nasty, smelly boat one moment longer. I won't, I won't, I WON'T.'

She stuck her head back behind the curtain of the Royal Procession Chair. 'Derek! Derek! Come out here and look where we are.'

'Who *is* she talking to?' asked Pancake.

They all watched as the stroppy princess drew back the curtains to reveal a third occupant in the Royal Procession Chair. The crew of the *Flying Pig* gasped in amazement.

'Who the—?' began Portia.

'This is my twin brother, Derek,' explained
Poppy. 'We go everywhere together. I can't believe
you slept through all this rumpus,' she said
looking at her brother. 'Derek!' she added
dramatically. 'We've been kidnapped!'

'Nonsense! said Portia angrily. 'Look, here's the
letter you sent me.' She shoved it under Poppy's nose.

'How many times do I have to tell you
I didn't write to you. Why would I? I like being
a princess.' She glanced at the letter. 'It's not
my writing anyway. You'll just have to take
us home.'

'Impossible!' said Portia. 'You'll have to stay
on board until we can drop you off somewhere
where we won't be arrested. Now pipe down
before I lose my temper!'

Derek stomped over and sneered at Portia.

'Don't you DARE speak to my sister like that,' he snarled. 'And anyway, who put you in charge? You're just a girl!'

There was another huge gasp from the crew of the *Flying Pig*. Portia looked as though she was about to explode.

'That's IT!' she roared. 'I've had just about enough! Jim.'

'Yes, Cap'n,' said Jim.

'Take them below and tell them how we run things around here.'

Jim stepped forward and hurried the disagreeable pair away.

'Daddy will send a ship to rescue us, just you wait and see,' said Poppy, as she was led down the stairs of the main deck.

Jim showed the Prince and Princess around the ship.

'We all have different jobs to do on board,' he explained. 'So we'll find something for you both to do while you're here.' He took them below. 'Here are the crew's sleeping quarters.'

Jim looked at Princess Poppy, who wore a look of complete horror on her face.

'This place is horrid,' she wailed. 'It's dusty, filthy and disgusting. *And* it smells of sweaty feet. Doesn't anyone ever clean up or decorate around here? Yuck!' She brushed a cobweb from her hair.

Jim looked around feeling a little ashamed.

'Hmmm. I suppose it has got a bit ... er shabby.' Then he had a bright idea. 'Why don't you sort it out while you're here? I'm sure the others would lend a hand when they're not too busy.'

Poppy looked around the sleeping quarters and thought for a moment. She'd always wanted to decorate the palace but King Colin wouldn't allow it. It might be fun to make the ship a nicer place to be, and after all, she might as well do something to pass the time until she returned to the palace.

'Very well,' said Poppy. 'But I'll need an assistant.'

Excellent!' said Jim. 'And what about you, Prince Derek?'

'I'm not doing *anything*,' growled Derek. 'Don't have to at the palace. Don't have to here,' he sneered.

'I'm afraid you'll have to do something,' said Jim crossly. 'That's if you want to be fed.'

'Yeah, yeah, yeah,' yawned Derek, rudely. 'Now leave me alone,' he said, climbing into a hammock. 'I'm going to take a nap.'

Chapter Four

Back at the palace, King Colin was hopping mad.

'WHO DOES THIS PRINCESS PORTIA THINK SHE IS?!!' he bellowed. 'HOW DARE SHE RUIN THE ROYAL PLANS!'

If he was completely honest, he had to admit that he was crosser about being made to look foolish in front of his people than he was about Princess Poppy being taken off by Portia.

At the other end of the throne room sat Queen Bettina, blubbing her eyes out.

'Oh, the shame! The embarrassment!' she sobbed. 'We'll have to send all the wedding presents back. It's a calamity!'

Meanwhile, Crown Prince Englebert was being comforted by Princess Daisy, Poppy's younger sister. She had always had a soft spot for Englebert. She, too, was a keen Morris Dancer and she had a very decent collection of buttons herself.

'Oh, my poor Princey,' cooed Daisy. 'Let me cheer you up. Come and see my button collection. Maybe we can do some swaps.'

'Ooh yeth pleathe,' said Prince Englebert. 'That would be terwiffic!' He trotted off cheerfully with Princess Daisy. He'd actually always preferred her to her sister!

A tall dark figure stepped forward, walked over to King Colin and bowed very low.

'Ah, Count Nasty! You got my message,' said King Colin.

'Yes, your Majesty,' Count Nasty said with an evil grin.

'We will sail after them immediately,' said King Colin. 'Have Lord Admiral Snatchett prepare our fastest ship.'

'I've seen to that already, your Majesty,' said Count Nasty slimily. 'We'll be ready to sail at dawn. Don't worry, Princess Portia will not escape me this time.'

King Colin clapped him hard on the back.

'Good work, Count Nasty!' he boomed. 'Get me back my daughter and you'll be a very rich man. Bettina, my dear, stop that snivelling and have the servants prepare our things. We're going on a little voyage.'

'We?' asked Count Nasty, slightly concerned. 'You mean you're coming too, your Majesty?'

'Absolutely!' said King Colin. 'And the Queen, Princess Daisy and, of course, the Crown Prince will all be accompanying me. Come along, my dear,' he said to Queen Bettina, shuffling her out of the throne room. 'All is not lost, we'll get our little Poppy back. That reminds me, where is Prince Derek? I haven't seen him since this morning.

I suppose he's asleep somewhere, the lazy boy. . .
Oh well, no time to search for him now, too much
to do. . .' King Colin prattled on as they left the
room.

'Oh terrific!' Count Nasty said to himself,
sarcastically. 'Just what I need, a ship full of
royalty.' He took out his pocket watch and
checked the time. 'Well, Princess Portia, I'm
coming to get you soon. And *this* time you'll
not escape.'

Chapter Five

The next morning was bright and sunny and on board the *Flying Pig*, Princess Poppy was rather enjoying herself.

'OK, ladies,' she said to the team of cleaners she'd assembled. 'Let's get to work!'

With the help of Bosun Betty, she'd scoured the ship for all the cleaning equipment she could find, and then organised her helpers into teams of two or three. They cleaned, swept and polished the ship from top to bottom. The most disgusting mess was put into sealed barrels ready to dispose of at the next port. Anything that could be re-used or recycled was either washed or stored away and, by the late afternoon, the team of cleaners was exhausted but happy.

'Wow!' exclaimed Portia, when she examined the results of all their hard work. 'You've done a fantastic job!'

'They've been a great team!' said Poppy. 'All it took was a little bit of organisation.'

'I can't believe how grubby we'd let it get,' said Bosun Betty. 'But Princess Poppy has given us some great tips for keeping on top of the mess.'

'This is only the beginning,' said Poppy excitedly. 'I've worked out a schedule for washing all the bedclothes *and* the hammocks, but we need to organise some more storage space.

Donnatella tells me that everyone's old dresses
and petticoats are packed away somewhere on
the ship and I have plans for those too.' She was
positively bursting with enthusiasm. 'Here, I've
made some drawings of what we might be able
to do.' Poppy showed Portia a notebook that
she'd borrowed from Pandora.

   'Good gracious!' said Portia, amazed. 'You have
been busy!'

   'Yes, I know,' Poppy giggled. 'It's been really
good fun. I don't know *how* I'll get it all done
before I have to go home, so if you'll excuse me, I
must get on!' She whizzed off dragging
Donnatella behind her. 'OK, Donnatella, take me
to Pandora's workshop and then show me where
the dresses are.'

Derek, on the other hand, had been totally unhelpful. He'd spent almost the entire day dozing, with Froo-Froo on his lap. The small hairy dog was still avoiding Twiggy and, with Poppy tearing around the ship like a maniac, Derek was his safest option. The only time Derek had moved was when the cleaning team disturbed him, at which point, he simply found a sunny spot on the deck to laze instead.

'You're going to have to do *something*,' scowled Peppermint at the lazy good-for-nothing prince.

'Not a chance,' said Derek, relaxing in the hot sun. 'I'm a prince, I don't have to.'

'You're going to get very hungry then,' said Pandora, walking past with her tool kit. 'And just you wait 'til you smell Pancake's cooking.'

'Hmmph!' grunted Derek.

Earlier in the day, Poppy had smuggled him a little breakfast, but by lunchtime, she too was beginning to get annoyed.

'Come on, Derek, it wouldn't do you any harm to do a little work. You might even enjoy it. It's actually nice to do something useful for a change,' she said.

'You ARE joking, I hope,' he sneered.

'Well, don't expect me to bring you any lunch, I'll be far too busy. Anyway, I don't see why I should give you any more of my food, not when I'm working so hard.' And off Poppy flounced.

By the evening, when delicious smells began to come from the galley, Derek's stomach really began to rumble. He felt so hungry that it was as if his stomach was trying to eat itself! Very reluctantly, he went to speak to Portia, who was chatting to his sister.

'OK, you win,' said Derek. 'If I help out around the ship tomorrow, will you let me have some dinner?'

Portia smiled a little smugly.

'It might help if you said *please*,' she said.

'All right, all right! If I *promise* to help out around the ship tomorrow, *please* may I have some dinner?'

'What do you think, Poppy?' Portia asked the Princess. 'Can we trust him?'

'I'm sure he'll be helpful tomorrow,' said Poppy. 'Please let him join us for dinner.'

'Very well,' agreed Portia. 'Since Poppy's been so brilliant today, but you'll have to work very hard. Go down to the galley and tell Pancake I sent you.'

Derek sloped off followed by Froo-Froo, who was hoping for some scraps.

'I'll help all right,' Derek said to himself, smiling. 'But you'll probably wish I hadn't!'

The next morning, Poppy was already hard at work when Portia emerged from her cabin. She was surrounded by piles of fabrics and colour swatches, and was having a whale of a time.

'Morning, Poppy,' said Portia, stretching and yawning. 'How are you today?'

'Very busy actually,' she replied unclearly
because she had a mouth full of coloured pencils.
'What do you think?'

Poppy showed Portia the designs she'd been
working on and Portia was very impressed.

'I discussed the plans with Pandora yesterday,
and she and Jim are going to help with the
carpentry. By the way, are they up yet?'

'Having breakfast,' Portia replied. 'And where's
that lazy brother of yours? I've got plenty of jobs
for him to do today.'

'He's just taking Froo-Froo for a walk around the deck. He'll be back in a minute,' said Poppy, getting back to work.

Portia marched off to find Derek. Just as she suspected, he hadn't got very far with the walk and was actually lounging on a pile of ropes, eating toast. Froo-Froo was on his lap catching the crumbs. Unfortunately for Derek, he was sitting directly below the ship's bell, so Portia sneaked past him up the steps and rang the bell as loudly as she could.

'YAAARRRGH! What's going on?!' yelled Derek, leaping to his feet, his heart racing. Froo-Froo went flying. The rest of the crew appeared on deck summoned by the bell.

'Sorry everyone!' chuckled Portia. 'I couldn't resist it — he looked so peaceful. Anyway, Derek, now you're on your feet, you can help Peppermint and the others swab the decks.'

'Oh goody,' said Derek. 'I can't wait.' He whispered to Froo-Froo, 'Just because I said I'd work, doesn't mean to say I'll be very good at it, eh, Froo-Froo?' He poked his tongue out at Portia as she walked away.

'Here,' said Peppermint, thrusting a mop into his hands. 'Make yourself useful.'

For twenty minutes, Derek followed Peppermint, Anisha and Claire around, not trying at all hard to clean anything. He even managed to cover Squawk in mucky water.

'Oops, sorry!' he said, tripping Anisha up with
his mop. 'Oh, clumsy me!' he went on, poking
Claire accidentally-on-purpose in the stomach.

'You're dangerous, you are!' moaned Anisha,
rubbing a sore elbow.

'Go and empty the buckets and get some
fresh water,' said Peppermint, as she helped
Claire to her feet. While they weren't watching,
Derek, pretending to trip, tipped the four buckets
of dirty water all over the newly washed deck.

'DEREK!!!' groaned the others in unison.

'That's it,' said Peppermint crossly. 'Clearly you're no good at cleaning. Go and see Portia so she can find you something else to do.'

'Yes, of course, Peppermint! Sorry about the mess,' he trotted off, sniggering.

Derek's next job was helping Pancake in the galley. She was normally a very patient teacher but Derek soon drove her nuts.

'OK, Derek, I know you've probably hardly ever set foot in a kitchen so I won't give you anything very complicated to do,' she said. 'Nancy and I are preparing food for this evening's feast so it's going to be busy in here all day. If you could just keep an eye on lunch, that would be terrific.'

'No problem,' said Derek enthusiastically.

Lunch was soup, two kinds: spicy pumpkin and cream of tomato. Both smelled delicious and Prince Derek couldn't help himself. He spent just as much time tasting as he did stirring. Then he spotted a large pot of chilli powder on the shelf near the stove.

While Pancake and Nancy's backs were turned, Derek accidentally-on-purpose knocked it into the spicy pumpkin soup.

'Oh no! Oh dear! What have I done?' he exclaimed, quickly stirring it in so the soup could not be salvaged.

Pancake rushed over.

'Oh no! There's no time to make a fresh batch now,' she said, tasting the soup gingerly. 'Yeuch! That'd blow everyone's heads off if I served it.'

'I'm *so* sorry,' said Derek sincerely. 'That was *really* clumsy. I won't have any soup for lunch so at least it will go a little bit further.'

'Judging by the soup stains on his shirt, he won't need any lunch anyway,' Nancy whispered to Pancake.

'I think you'd better find another job to do,' said Pancake. 'I'll get someone else to help.'

'All right then, I'll go and find the Captain,' said Derek, and off he went smirking.

Derek was sent to help Jim, Pandora and Sophie, who were building shelves and storage units to Poppy's designs.

'Ooopsie!' said Derek when he nailed two pieces of wood to the deck "by mistake". 'I don't think I'm very good at DIY. I always came bottom in woodwork class.'

'Thanks for warning us!' said Jim.

'Here,' Pandora said more patiently. 'Hammer this while I hold the edges together.'

Derek tapped happily with the hammer, then accidentally on purpose tapped Pandora's thumb instead.

'YOWWWWW!!' yelled Pandora, hopping around holding her thumb in agony.
'Ooops!' said Prince Derek.

His last job of the day was to help Bosun Betty and some of the crew with repairs to the sails. Once again he managed to sabotage the job. Worse than that, the sail he was supposed to be repairing ended up with a rip from top to bottom.

'I'm sorry, I'm not very good at sewing,' said Derek lamely.

'This is a disaster,' said Bosun Betty. 'It's really going to slow us down.'

Derek smiled slyly.

By the end of the day, half the crew had been to see Portia to complain about Derek. Even Squawk joined in.

'Disastrous Derek! Disastrous Derek!' squawked Squawk.

'He's hopeless!' said Bosun Betty.

'He just can't do anything right,' agreed Nancy.

'We were better off when he did nothing,' grumbled Pandora, nursing her bandaged thumb.

'Isn't there somewhere we could shove him where he can't do any damage?' pleaded Peppermint.

'Send him in,' sighed Portia.

Derek entered Portia's cabin trying to look as though he felt really guilty for messing things up.

'I was trying to be helpful,' he whinged. 'I just haven't had much practice.'

'Yes, so it would seem,' said Portia slowly. 'I think you'd better go up in the crow's nest and keep watch until the feast starts at dusk. And take that fluffy thing with you. I'm sick of Twiggy chasing it around the ship.'

'Absolutely. Right away!' said Derek. He turned and walked away, rubbing his hands together. Froo-Froo was waiting outside.

'Come on, you hairy mutt, you're coming with me.'

As Prince Derek climbed up to the crow's nest with Froo-Froo under one arm, he was feeling really smug.

'Well, Froo-Froo,' he said, 'everything is going brilliantly! I've managed to mess things up *and* slow us down, so Daddy's ship should be catching us up by now. Won't Count Nasty be impressed! Mind you, if I hadn't thought of forging the letter to Portia in the first place, he would never have come up with the plan. It's a good job that she didn't look any closer at the writing though or she might have recognised it.'

Froo-Froo looked at the Prince, then down at the deck which was getting further and further away. He squeezed his eyes tight shut and clung on for dear life.

'All we've got to do now,' Derek continued, 'is look out for Daddy's ship and make sure no one else spots it.'

They reached the crow's nest and Derek glanced casually around, just in case someone below might be watching him. A tiny speck was visible on the horizon and he had to try really hard to suppress a squeal of delight. Derek took out the telescope to get a better look.

'Hee hee!' Derek chuckled quietly. 'There they are, right on schedule!' He put the telescope down quickly so that nobody saw him looking out to sea and glanced below at the activity on deck.

Poppy was still beavering away. She seemed happier than he had ever seen her. However unpleasant a character he was, Derek loved his twin sister dearly and seeing her so happy made him smile.

'I wonder why she's having so much fun,' he said to himself. 'She never looks that happy at the palace.'

Delicious food smells floated up from the galley and reached Derek's nose right up high in the crow's nest.

'Yumm!' Derek hummed. 'Something smells incredible!' He leant against the mast, closed his eyes and dozed off.

An hour later, Derek was woken by the ship's bell.

'Feast time! Feast time!' announced Peppermint.

'Derek! Froo-Froo!' called Princess Poppy from below. 'Come and join the party.'

The table looked beautiful. Poppy had made a huge tablecloth and everyone had a napkin folded to look like a swan. By the time Derek and Froo-Froo reached the deck, everyone had taken their place. Poppy had saved a seat for Derek next to her, and Froo-Froo was given a bowl nearby, well away from Squawk and Twiggy.

Portia rose to make a toast.

'I know this isn't a normal welcome feast because Poppy and Derek won't be staying. We'll be approaching a friendly port in a day or so and will have to say goodbye to them both.'

There were cries of 'shame' and 'she should stay' when Portia mentioned Poppy, but silence when she spoke of Derek. Poppy was obviously really chuffed that the crew had grown to like her so much. Portia went on.

'But I thought we should have a celebration to show our appreciation of what a fantastic job Poppy has done on the ship!'

There was a huge cheer and the whole crew stamped their feet and banged on the table to make as much noise as possible. Derek felt really proud of her.

'Speech!' called Pandora.

Poppy got to her feet.

'Thank you, thank you everyone. You're very kind!' said Poppy blushing. 'I'd just like to say that I've enjoyed my time on board, and it's a shame I won't have time to complete all my plans.' The crew murmured agreement. 'But if Daddy, I mean King Colin, should catch us up or capture Portia, I will make him promise not to send you all back!'

There was a huge cheer of approval from everyone except Derek, who was beginning to feel a little uneasy.

'OK, everyone,' said Portia when the cheers died down. 'Tuck in! It's time to party.'

They all had a great time. Even Derek began to enjoy himself and Twiggy, Squawk and Froo-Froo seemed to have decided not to fight any more.

Emily played the accordion and everyone danced
and sang. Then later on, Portia organised some
party games. They played Blind Pirate's Buff,
Musical Bumps, Musical Statues (with forfeits).
There were races up and down the masts, and
from one end of the ship to the other, and by
special request, Poppy's favourite game,
Charades.

'If Daddy comes to rescue us,' Poppy said to
Portia. 'I won't let him throw you in jail.'

'He'd have to catch me first!' hooted Portia,
swinging tarzan-like from mast to mast.

Poppy laughed.

'This is the *best* party ever!' she said.

It was very late by the time the party came to
an end.

'I'll keep watch tonight, Captain,' Derek
offered. 'It'll make up for all the trouble I caused
today.'

'That's very kind of you, Derek,' replied Portia. 'It's good to see you're settling in at last. Jim will send someone to take over in the morning, but don't forget to sound the alarm if you see anything unusual.'

'Yes, Captain,' said Derek. 'Sleep well.'

Portia went off to bed and Prince Derek began the climb up to the crow's nest. Of course, the only reason that Derek had offered to keep watch, was to make sure that no one else spotted his father's ship. He picked up the telescope and looked out to sea. Although it was midnight, there was a full moon and a clear sky, and there in the distance he could see King Colin's ship, the *Blue Falcon*.

'Heh heh heh, there you are!' Derek said quietly to himself. 'Closer and closer!' He sat down in the crow's nest, curled up and went to sleep.

Chapter Eight

In the morning, the entire ship was awoken by Jim's frantic cries.

'Ship ahoy! Ship ahoy! All hands on deck. It's an emergency!!' he shouted ringing the ship's bell furiously.

The Captain and crew emerged sleepy-eyed onto the main deck.

'What's going on, Jim?' asked Portia, rushing to join him on the poop deck.

'It's King Colin's ship,' said Jim, handing her the telescope. 'And I think Count Nasty's on board!'

Portia focused the telescope and, just as Jim had feared, she saw the evil face of Count Nasty staring back at her. She turned to the crew.

'Hoist the main sail and weigh anchor. Get up as much speed as you can. She'll be on us within the hour. And bring me that lazy Prince Derek. He's got a lot of explaining to do.'

But Derek was already on his way down from the crow's nest. He swaggered over to Portia with a huge grin on his face.

'Why do you think I offered to keep watch?' he said spitefully. 'You didn't think I actually wanted to be *helpful* did you? In fact, our plan has all gone very smoothly from the start.'

'Plan! You mean you and Poppy— ?' began Portia.

'Oh no, Poppy knew nothing about it. Me and the Count, of course. I wrote the letter that brought you to rescue her, and Count Nasty had the *Blue Falcon* ready to follow.'

Everybody gasped in horror.

'*You* wrote to Portia?' exclaimed Poppy, staring in amazement at her brother. 'But why, Derek? What has she ever done to you?'

'She's been making life hell for us princes. No one knows if there'll even be any princesses left before long. So I got in touch with Count Nasty and we hatched this plan. My job was to get us on the ship and slow it down so that he can catch all the princesses together. Clever, eh?'

'Why you—' started Peppermint. 'Captain, we should throw him overboard.' The crew agreed.

'Wait!' said Poppy. 'Please don't. He can't swim. I'm . . . I'm really sorry about all this.' She turned to her brother. 'Derek, how could you be so deceitful?'

'Well, you're responsible for him now, Poppy. Make sure he gets up to no more treachery,' said Portia. She turned back to the crew. 'What are you waiting for? Get the rest of the sails up and get us moving as fast as we can go. Jim, Peppermint, Pandora, Betty, we need to work out what to do.'

They went off to Portia's cabin, leaving Poppy and Derek alone on the poop deck. Derek looked back at his father's ship and took a long, deep breath.

'Back to a life of luxury,' he said contentedly. 'I can't wait.'

Poppy, too, was looking back but her expression was different from her brother's. She was having so much fun, she wasn't actually sure if she wanted to go back to being a princess.

Chapter Nine

Derek looked at Poppy.

'What's the matter?' he asked. 'You look really unhappy. Aren't you excited about going home?'

Poppy stared out to sea.

'I know I should be, but I'm not at all sure I *want* to go back,' she sniffed. 'I'm having such a nice time. I've made some real friends and I never get to do anything this interesting back at the palace.'

'But I thought you'd be pleased,' said Derek. 'You said you liked being a princess.'

'Yes I did,' Poppy replied, 'but that was before. I like it *here* now and I would hate it if they got into trouble because of us.'

Derek suddenly felt awful because he'd made his sister unhappy and, if he were entirely honest, he was getting to like the crew the more time he spent on board. He knew the seafaring life was not for him, but they obviously all enjoyed it.

'If only there was something we could do to help,' said Poppy mournfully.

In Portia's cabin, they were wracking their brains for a way out of their predicament.

'Any ideas?' asked Portia hopefully.

'Well, we're too far away from any friendly ports for that to be an option,' said Jim, studying the charts.

'We still have the giant catapult. I tested it the other day and it's working fine,' said Pandora.

'Yes, but we've no ammunition,' moaned Peppermint.

Pancake entered the cabin with a large breakfast tray and put it down between them.

'Can we outrun them?' she asked.

'Not for long,' Portia replied gloomily, 'They're bigger and faster than us. I'm afraid we're done for this time.'

'Maybe if we just gave them back Poppy and Derek, Poppy could persuade them to let us go?' said Bosun Betty hopefully.

'Count Nasty would never let that happen. He's been after me for too long,' Portia said. 'But maybe if I give myself up he'll release the rest of you?'

'No! NEVER!' they all shouted.

'We're in this together,' said Peppermint, looking at the others.'Aren't we?'

They all nodded somberly.

Up on the poop deck, Poppy was pacing around trying to think of a way she could get Portia and the crew of the *Flying Pig* out of the situation that Derek had landed them in.

'Think, Derek think!' she said, shaking him by the shoulders. 'They're getting closer.'

Derek didn't know what to do. He wanted Poppy to be happy, but he wanted to go back home.

'But if we help Portia,' Derek pleaded, not that he had any bright ideas about how to do it, 'then we won't be able to go back.'

'Of course we will. Portia was going to drop us off somewhere safe soon anyway. We could make our own way home from there.'

'I suppose so,' said Derek hesitantly. He was beginning to feel a little guilty.

'I know there's no ammunition on board. Peppermint told me while we were doing our spring clean.' Poppy paused and looked at Derek. Suddenly her face lit up. 'That's it!' she exclaimed. 'I've got it. Come on, Derek. Let's find Portia.'

Chapter Ten

Poppy burst into Portia's cabin.

'I've got an idea,' she said. 'I think I know how we can see them off.'

'What do you mean?' asked Portia a little puzzled, 'I thought you wanted them to rescue you.'

'That's not important at the moment,' said Poppy. 'We need to get a move on, if this is going to work!'

'If what's going to work?' asked Jim.

'Quick, follow me. I'll show you!'

Poppy turned and ran out of the cabin and down the stairs of the main deck, with the others in pursuit.

'Where on earth is she taking us?' Portia asked Pancake, as they ran after Poppy.

They went down further, further into the deep, dark, smelliest part of the ship, the place where all the barrels of disgusting rubbish had been taken.

'Phew! It stinks down here!' said Jim, pinching his nose to keep out the smell.

There were forty-nine barrels all packed with revolting, stinking rubbish.

'This is it!' said Poppy.

'I don't understand,' said Portia, beginning to wonder if Poppy had gone mad.

'You can load it into the cannons!' said Poppy. They all looked blank. 'Use it as ammunition. It'll be disgusting!'

'That's pure genius!' said Portia, 'I can't wait to see their faces.' She hugged Poppy. 'Thanks shipmate,' she said.

Poppy was delighted.

'OK!' said Portia. 'Get everybody down here right away. Let's get this stuff moved.'

It took the whole crew to get the forty-nine barrels of smelly muck onto the main deck.

'There's the rubbish from yesterday's feast in barrels in the galley storeroom, too. We haven't had a chance to get rid of it,' said Pancake. 'There are fish bones, chicken bones, vegetable peelings and stuff. It's all mixed up with what we scraped off the plates and swept from the floor. Nancy and I will fetch those up, too.'

By the time all the barrels were on deck, King Colin's ship, the *Blue Falcon*, was within a ship's length of the *Flying Pig*. Portia could see the

familiar figure of Count Nasty, shouting orders at the crew.

'Right,' said Portia. 'There's not much time. All cover your noses. This is NOT going to be pleasant,' she warned, as she began to remove the barrel lids.

Old, mouldy bread, rotten fruit and vegetables, smelly socks and underpants, rotting fish and meat, all the rubbish that Poppy and her team of cleaners had collected – in fact, every kind of smelly, disgusting muck that you can think of –

was loaded into the cannons and the catapult. Some of it was scooped into buckets and passed around the crew for hand-to-hand fighting.

All too soon, the *Blue Falcon* was upon them, and its grappling hooks were swung across to the *Flying Pig*. It was time for battle.

Chapter Eleven

The last cannon was loaded just as King Colin's
men began to climb across the ropes towards
the *Flying Pig*.

'FIRE!!!' ordered Portia.

Gallons of rotten, disgusting muck and gloop
flew through the air and splattered King Colin's
men and their ship. The king himself was narrowly
missed by a blast of rotten eggs.

'Yeucchh!' shrieked Prince Englebert, as he was
struck by several squidgy banana skins at once. It
was quite revolting. For a moment, they were
completely stopped in their tracks by the stench
and the goo.

'Carry on, men, carry on!' roared Count Nasty, angrily shaking spaghetti from his beard. 'It can't hurt you, you fools. Hold your noses. The first man, who gets on board the *Flying Pig,* will be richly rewarded.'

Hearing this, King Colin's crew were spurred on. Some rowed across and began to climb up the hull of the ship.

'Fire!!' shouted Portia again.

A second barrage of muck flew through the air, and buckets of muck and smelly water landed on the men, who were climbing the hull. Some of them deliberately jumped into the sea to wash the nasty stuff off.

'It's working!' Poppy said to Derek, jumping up and down with glee. 'Isn't this exciting?!'

Derek was astounded.

On board the *Blue Falcon*, Count Nasty was beside himself with rage.

'You're all pathetic!' he hollered at King Colin's crew, who were cowering any place they could find cover, or jumping in the sea to get clean. The royal party itself had taken refuge in the Captain's cabin and were watching the goings-on from behind the door.

'It's a good job I brought some of my own men with me,' Count Nasty continued. 'Bill, Crusher, get the men together. We are boarding that ship if it's the last thing we do.' He stormed over to the *Blue Falcon's* remaining dinghy and climbed in, followed by his little band of thugs. 'Lower away,'

he ordered King Colin's men gruffly. 'And get a
move on or I'll have you all court-martialled.'

In moments, the dinghy was in the water and
heading towards the *Flying Pig*.

'Faster! Faster!' urged Count Nasty.

SPLAT! SQUELCH!! A load of smelly muck
landed in the middle of the boat and splashed all
the occupants.

'Yuck!'

'Earghh!'

'Yeuchhh!'

The *Flying Pig's* crew had hysterics and Portia
ran towards the end of the ship to get a better
look at the spectacle. But on her way, disaster
struck. She skidded on some gunge that had
leaked from a barrel and flew head first over the
side of the ship and into the sea!

There was total panic.

'Portia! Portia!' everyone shouted, as Count
Nasty's boat rowed towards her. She started
swimming back to the ship, as fast as she could,
but they were gaining on her.

'A golden sovereign for every man in the boat if we catch her!' said Count Nasty, feeling victory within his grasp.

The promise of cash did the trick and the men began to row like maniacs

'Quick, someone throw her a rope!' yelled Jim.

'Oh Derek! What are we going to do?' Poppy said, clinging to her brother. 'Portia will be captured and we'll be overrun.' She burst into tears.

'What do you mean, "we"?' he asked.

'I mean I want to stay here and be part of the crew. I don't want to go back and spend the rest of my days Morris Dancing and collecting buttons,' she said dramatically. 'And whatever happens to Portia and the others will be all our fault!' Poppy threw herself sobbing into Derek's arms.

He pushed her back gently and looked her straight in the eyes.

'You're *sure*. You're absolutely sure you want to stay?' he asked.

'Yes,' said Poppy. 'More sure than I have ever been about anything.'

'Well, if that's what you really want,' Derek said, hugging her tight. 'I'll have to make sure you get it!'

Derek then did the bravest thing he had ever done in his life. He sped across the deck, grabbed a small barrel of the most disgusting-looking muck he could find, and climbed a rope that hung from the mast. He swung on it to get it moving.

'Sorry about all the trouble I've caused,' he called to Portia, as he flew backwards and forwards. 'But I'm going to put it right!'

Letting go just at the right point (he hoped), he went flying through the air.

'Geronimo!!' he cried, and landed with a thump in the middle of Count Nasty's boat.

'What's going owp!' Count Nasty said, as in one swift movement, Prince Derek emptied the barrel of muck over his head and wedged it on tight. In the kafuffle, Portia made her escape and began to climb the rope that the crew had thrown to her.

'CEASEFIRE!!' Derek yelled holding up his arms in a prince-like way he'd never quite managed before. 'I am Prince Derek and I order everyone to return to the *Blue Falcon*,' he said masterfully.

There was a round of applause, whistling and cheering from all aboard the *Flying Pig,* and stunned silence from the *Blue Falcon*. Count Nasty, who was stuck in the barrel, could do nothing.

'Derek, my boy, I wondered where you had got to,' said King Colin, coming out of his hiding place. 'Where's Princess Poppy?'

'She's staying on board the *Flying Pig*, Father,' Derek told him.

'Nonsense! She must come home and marry Prince Englebert.'

'But, Daddy,' piped up Princess Daisy. 'Can't *I* marry Prince Englebert instead? I love him much more than Poppy does, and he loves me.'

'Is this true?' demanded the King.

'Oh yeth, thir!' said Prince Englebert earnestly, stepping forward happily and grabbing Daisy's hand. 'Pwintheth Daithy ith the girl of my dweams.'

'Well,' considered King Colin, smiling at his wife. 'I suppose if everyone agrees, and Poppy really wants to stay, the wedding can go ahead as soon as we return. Let the *Flying Pig* be on its way.'

There were cheers from both ships as the King made the announcement, but Count Nasty was still struggling to get out of the barrel.

'Thank you, Daddy!' called Poppy from the *Flying Pig*. 'I'll keep in touch!'

Chapter Twelve

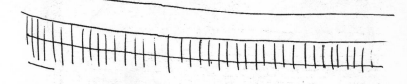

The *Flying Pig* was allowed to sail away peacefully. Derek still held on tight to Count Nasty and the barrel, while the crew of the *Blue Falcon* began their clean up.

Take care,' he said, waving goodbye to Poppy with a tear in his eye. 'I'll miss you.' Although Derek was sad, he knew he'd done a really good thing and it gave him a warm feeling inside, one that he'd never really felt before. 'It was fun!' he said to Portia, 'but much too much like hard work for a lazy bones like me.' And before he realised what he was doing, he blew her a kiss.

For the first time in her life, Portia blushed.

VOYAGES O

West

| Princess Peppermint of Pomerania | Princess Pandora of Patagonia | Princess Pancake of Pescado | Princess Poppy of Pimento |

Are you a
Princess in Peril?
Contact
Parrot Postbox 999
Portia The
Pirate Princess